Dear Parent:
Your child's love of reading starts here!

Every child learns to read in a different way and at his or her own speed. Some go back and forth between reading levels and read favorite books again and again. Others read through each level in order. You can help your young reader improve and become more confident by encouraging his or her own interests and abilities. From books your child reads with you to the first books he or she reads alone, there are I Can Read Books for every stage of reading:

SHARED READING
Basic language, word repetition, and whimsical illustrations, ideal for sharing with your emergent reader

BEGINNING READING
Short sentences, familiar words, and simple concepts for children eager to read on their own

READING WITH HELP
Engaging stories, longer sentences, and language play for developing readers

READING ALONE
Complex plots, challenging vocabulary, and high-interest topics for the independent reader

ADVANCED READING
Short paragraphs, chapters, and exciting themes for the perfect bridge to chapter books

I Can Read Books have introduced children to the joy of reading since 1957. Featuring award-winning authors and illustrators and a fabulous cast of beloved characters, I Can Read Books set the standard for beginning readers.

A lifetime of discovery begins with the magical words **"I Can Read!"**

Visit www.icanread.com for information
on enriching your child's reading experience.

For James, who loves to help
feed the pets!
—A.S.C.

I Can Read Book® is a trademark of HarperCollins Publishers.

Biscuit Feeds the Pets   Text copyright © 2016 by Alyssa Satin Capucilli Illustrations copyright © 2016 by Pat Schories
All rights reserved. Manufactured in China. No part of this book may be used or reproduced in any manner whatsoever without
written permission except in the case of brief quotations embodied in critical articles and reviews. For information address
HarperCollins Children's Books, a division of HarperCollins Publishers, 195 Broadway, New York, NY 10007.
www.icanread.com

Library of Congress Control Number: 2014041211
ISBN 978-0-06-223697-5 (hardcover) — ISBN 978-0-06-223696-8 (pbk.)

The artist used traditional watercolor to create the illustrations for this book.

15   16   17   18   19   SCP   10   9   8   7   6   5   4   3   2   1   ❖   First Edition

Biscuit Feeds the Pets

story by ALYSSA SATIN CAPUCILLI
pictures by PAT SCHORIES

HARPER
An Imprint of HarperCollinsPublishers

Here, Biscuit.

We're going to help

Mrs. Gray today.

Woof, woof!

3

We're going to help
feed the pets!

Are you ready, Biscuit?

Woof, woof!

We can help feed
the fish, Biscuit.

We can help feed
the kittens, too.
Woof, woof!
Meow!

Wait, Biscuit!

Where are you going?

Woof, woof!
Yip—yip—yip!

Oh, Biscuit.

You found the new puppies!

Woof!

This way, Biscuit.

Woof, woof!

There are more pets
to feed over here.

Woof!

Biscuit!

Come out of there.

It's not time to play.

It's time to help Mrs. Gray.

Woof!

Yip!

Oh no, Biscuit!

Come back.
How will we feed
the pets now?

Woof, woof!

Yip—yip—yip!

Meow!

No, Biscuit, no.

Not the water bowl!

SPLASH!
Silly puppies!

Woof, woof!
Yip—yip—yip!

Funny puppy!

You found your own way to
help feed the pets, Biscuit.

You made lots of
new friends, too!

Meow!

Yip—yip—yip!

Woof, woof!

25